T0198880

The
Cuckoo Clock
& The
Grumbling Gear

Photo by: Ruby Gunn

Written by: Jeannie Bergland

To order additional copies of this book, contact:
Xlibris
844-714-8691
www.Xlibris.com
Orders@Xlibris.com

ISBN: Softcover   978-1-6698-7238-2
               EBook   978-1-6698-7237-5

Print information available on the last page

Rev. date: 03/29/2023

The Cuckoo Clock & The Grumbling Gear

The Clock Master, with a very steady hand and an eye for detail, was pleased with his work. He dusted off the sawdust and added his final touch to it. "Ah, it is very good", he said as he looked at it again. "It is complete. Now, to get it started." He took a key out to wind it up and listened to each turn and then carefully set it in it's place on the wall.

Once he had wound the clock up and set it in its place, something amazing happened - it came to life!

All the gears and gadgets inside begin to move, sing, and talk to one another. What a joy and delight it brought its creator, the Clock Master!

One last look, and a little more oil for the gears, so that everything will operate smoothly.

The Master then closed the door. The clock had everything it needed to function correctly. The Clock Master was pleased with all his hard work.

The clock functioned for many years, as it was designed to do.

Then one day, one of the small gears in the darkest part of the clock became tired of doing the same thing over and over. It soon began to doubt its purpose and spoke out to its neighboring parts asking, "What are we doing here? I'm tired of doing the same old thing all of the time!"

The parts that were close by were just as much in the dark as this small gear. They soon began to doubt and question what their purpose was too. Once they were all happy and working all together in unison. Now, they began to complain and everything came to a halt! The Clock Master was concerned. It should not have stopped working. He took a key to wind it up and it started to work again; but something was different this time.

Inside the beautiful clock, parts begin having a discussion concerning their purpose. The little grumbling gear spoke out of its darkness and began to tell the other parts that it thought they could change jobs and positions in the clock and everything would be fine.

Nearly all the parts agreed! After all, they were all in this dark world together and seemed to be doing a great job on their own. Nearly all of them were tired of doing the same old thing over and over too.

Just then the Cuckoo bird chimed in and said, "Wait a minute! I have seen the outside and there is a light! We were all made by the Clock Master and we all have a purpose in here. We were made to be a joy and a delight to him. We wouldn't be here if it were not for the Master."

One of the parts shouted back at the bird, "Oh yeah?! We don't see any "Master" and we are not seeing any "light" either!"

The arm that stretches out the bird responded, "I have seen the light. I have seen glimpses of the Clock Master and have heard his voice. I believe the word of the bird. It is true."

The key hole spoke up and said, "I have not seen much light, but something is out there that is greater than us in here. Every time we slow down or stop, something or someone comes just as everything becomes completely dark and no light can be seen. Something or someone moves and then something inside us clicks and we all begin to work again. Maybe it is the "Clock Master" or maybe it isn't, but there is definitely something outside of us that keeps us going. Maybe, we should look into and observe this light."

Another piece exclaims, "You almost sound like the bird! Whose side are you on? We move because we will it. We have power to move and power to stop moving, all on our own! We are powerful. It is because we all work together. It is because of us that the bird is able to go outside. As far as I am concerned it can stay outside! Besides, I have got glimpses of the light and it hurts my eyes. If there were a Clock Master, why would he allow something in here that would hurt us or cause us pain?"

Another part spoke up and responded, "Maybe, the light would not hurt your eyes if you allowed the light in. I'm close by where the light comes in and I think it is beautiful, and it gives me hope."

The little grumbling gear responded, "Hope?! Are you kidding me? I have hope too. It is not in the light or in some strange idea that someone or something is outside of where we live and is greater than us. If there were a "Clock Master", we could work together and be greater than him. We could make our own clocks and even better! We certainly would not allow in any light that would cause us pain!"

12

The cuckoo bird spoke up once again, "The light is not painful, if you spend time in it. Light is actually beautiful and helps one to see the Master better and his beautiful world. We wouldn't be here if it weren't for him. He made all of us and gave us the ability to do our jobs. He gave us life and I want to serve him joyfully. We should work together. The way we were created and designed to work. We all have a purpose and it is a good one. I trust the Master."

With that being said, most all of the parts agreed but some didn't and the clock didn't work right.

The Master came by with his tools and opened up the clock. All of the parts could see the light then!

The Clock Master removed the broken and rebellious parts, fixed what could be repaired; but the grumbling gear in the dark, got removed and thrown away.

Printed in the United States
by Baker & Taylor Publisher Services